# BLAST OFF, BAREFOOT BEAR!

ISBN  0-8300-0339-8

***Blast Off, Barefoot Bear!***
was prepared and produced by
Tern Enterprises, Inc.
Sagaponack Road
Bridgehampton, New York 11932

Cover and book design by Duncan S. McKenzie

Printed and bound in Hong Kong
by Leefung-Asco Printers Ltd.

Barefoot Bear™ is a trademark of
Tern Enterprises, Inc., Bridgehampton, New York

Produced exclusively for **Kaleidoscope**

# BLAST OFF, BAREFOOT BEAR!

by Lyn Calder
Illustrated by Kathy Allert

KALEIDOSCOPE

The early morning sunlight poured in through
Barefoot Bear's window, waking him. Barefoot Bear
slipped his hand under his pillow. He felt something
smooth and round and hard.

"Mom!" cried Barefoot Bear. "The tooth fairy was here!" Barefoot Bear held up a shiny quarter.

"That's because you are such a good little bear," said his mother.

Barefoot Bear ran to his mirror and grinned. "I may be a good little bear," he said, "but now I'm a funny-looking bear, too."

"You look fine, dear," said his mother as she hugged him. "Now, did you think about how you would like to spend your quarter?"

"I want to ride the Moon Rocket. Can I ride it today?" asked Barefoot Bear.

"As soon as we get dressed and eat our breakfast, we can go," answered Barefoot Bear's mother.
"Hurray!" shouted Barefoot Bear.

"Would you like some toast for breakfast?" asked Barefoot Bear's mother.

"Yes," said Barefoot Bear, "with honey on top."

Barefoot Bear looked at his reflection in the toaster.

"Don't worry," said his mother. "Before you know it, a new big-bear tooth will grow in."

The toast popped up, and Barefoot Bear sat down to eat his breakfast.

When they got to the Moon Rocket there was a long line. Barefoot Bear went to the end and waited.

Along came Raccoon. "Hi, Barefoot Bear," he said.
"How are you?"
"I lost my tooth yesterday!" said Barefoot Bear.
"Look!" Raccoon looked. Then he started to laugh.
"What's so funny?" asked Barefoot Bear.

"You are! You look funny without your tooth," Raccoon said.

Barefoot Bear turned his back on Raccoon. He felt the empty space where his tooth had been. "I'm not smiling again until this tooth grows back," he thought.

"Tickets, please!" said Mr. Badger. Barefoot Bear
handed Mr. Badger his ticket.

"You're the last one for this ride," said Mr. Badger.
Barefoot Bear left Raccoon waiting and headed for the
ride.

Red Rocket number three was empty. "That's my favorite!" said Barefoot Bear. He strapped himself in and listened for the countdown. "Three, two, one . . . Blast off!" called Mr. Badger.

The rockets went up, up in the air. Barefoot Bear
waved to his mother down below. Then he settled back in
his seat, closed his eyes . . .

. . . and headed for the moon.

The spaceship landed with a thud. Barefoot Bear
climbed out and began to explore. Then he turned and
saw a big red ball floating his way.

"Catch!" called a faraway voice. Barefoot Bear lifted his arms and caught the ball. "Now throw it back," called the faraway voice.

"I can't see you," said Barefoot Bear. "Where should I throw it?"

"I'm right here," said the voice. Barefoot Bear threw the ball. It must have traveled far because Barefoot Bear could not see where it landed.

"Good throw!" said the voice. "Who are you? And where are you from?"

"I'm Barefoot Bear from Earth. Who are you?" Barefoot Bear called back.

In the blink of an eye, a creature appeared. "I'm Malcolm," the creature said and took a little bow. Barefoot Bear bowed, too. But he was careful not to smile. He did not want Malcolm to laugh at him the way Raccoon had.

"My friends and I are playing a game," said Malcolm. "Do you want to play with us?"

"I'd like to," said Barefoot Bear, "but I don't see them."

"Take my hand," Malcolm said. "We'll find them in no time." Barefoot Bear took Malcolm's hand, and before he knew it, they were sailing off.

They landed in the middle of a group of creatures that looked very much like Malcolm.

"Say hello to Barefoot Bear, everyone," Malcolm said.

Malcolm's friends bowed. One stepped forward. "I'm Katie. Do you want to play "Shooting Star" with us?"

"I never played that game. Will you teach me?"

"Sure," said Katie.

The game was like "Tag." The player who was the shooting star was "it" and had to tag the rest. Barefoot Bear got to be the shooting star first.

"That was fun!" said Barefoot Bear when the game was over.

Barefoot Bear took the ball and taught his new friends
how to play "Hot Potato." They liked the game a lot and
wanted Barefoot Bear to teach them another.

"I'd like to," said Barefoot Bear, "but I think I'd better be getting back now."

"I'll take you to your ship," said Malcolm.

Barefoot Bear took Malcolm's hand and they were back at the ship in an instant. "Thanks for letting me play with you. I had a good time," Barefoot Bear said.

"Are you sure?" asked Malcolm. "You haven't smiled at all. Don't they smile where you come from?"

Barefoot Bear told Malcolm how he had lost his tooth and how Raccoon had laughed at him. "Losing a tooth is no big deal," said Malcolm. "We lose them all the time here. Look how loose this one is."

Malcolm wiggled his front tooth. He wiggled it so much that it fell out! Malcolm laughed. "See? Now we look the same," he said.

Barefoot Bear smiled. It was a big, happy smile. "Thanks, Malcolm," he said.

Malcolm waved. "Good-bye, Barefoot Bear. Come back soon!"

Barefoot Bear strapped himself in and blasted off for
Earth. Visiting the moon was fun, but it would be good
to be back home again.

When Barefoot Bear came out of the Moon Rocket, he was still smiling. He passed Raccoon who had been waiting and thinking.

"I'm sorry I laughed at you, Barefoot Bear," Raccoon said. "Will you still be my friend?"

Barefoot Bear said that he would be. Then he whispered to Raccoon, "Take Red Rocket number three. It's the best!"

Barefoot Bear ran to his mother. "I had fun on the moon!" he said.

"I had fun, too," said Barefoot Bear's mother. "I played a game and look what I won for you."

Barefoot Bear's mother handed him a big red ball.

Barefoot Bear looked up at the sky and smiled.